MEGA POWERS

CAN SCIENCE FACT DEFEAT SCIENCE FICTION?

WRITTEN BY

JACK WEYLAND!

ILLUSTRATED BY

KEN STEACY!

ADDISON-WESLEY
PUBLISHING COMPANY, INC.
Reading, Massachusetts
Menlo Park, California
New York   Don Mills, Ontario
Wokingham, England
Amsterdam   Bonn   Sydney
Singapore   Tokyo
Madrid   San Juan
Paris   Seoul   Milan
Mexico City   Taipei

24

To Sherry, for teaching me all the really important things in life.

ACKNOWLEDGEMENTS

Thanks to Kristi Foster for doing a wonderful job in developing hands-on activities. Thanks also to Jim Mears and Dr. Dennis Nesbit for going over the final manuscript.

Library of Congress Cataloging-in-Publication Data

Weyland, Jack, 1940–
    Megapowers : can science fact defeat science fiction? / written by Jack Weyland ; illustrated by Ken Steacy.
        p. cm.
    Includes index.
    Summary: Explores the truth behind science fiction phenomena such as x-ray eyes, invisibility, megastrength, etc., by examining the scientific facts.
    ISBN 0-201-58115-9
    1. Science—Juvenile literature. 2. Science—Experiments— Juvenile literature. [1. Science.] I. Steacy, Ken, ill. II. Title.
Q163.W44 1992
500—dc20   92-5441
                                        CIP
                                        AC

Text copyright © 1992 by Jack Weyland
Illustrations copyright © 1992 by Ken Steacy

Originally published by Kids Can Press, Ltd., of Toronto, Ontario, Canada.

Edited by Valerie Wyatt
Cover type design by Eileen Hoff
Book design by May Scobie
Set in 12-point Century Book by Leading Type

1 2 3 4 5 6 7 8 9–AL–95949392
First printing, May 1992

Text stock contains over 50% recycled paper

CONTENTS

OUR STORY BEGINS...

WITH THE ARRIVAL OF THE LATEST ISSUE OF YOUR FAVOURITE COMIC! WILL THE EVIL DR. GORK SUCCEED IN HIS EVIL PLOT TO TAKE OVER THE WORLD? OR WILL THE KID USE MEGAPOWERS AND SAVE THE DAY? TURN THE PAGE AND FIND OUT!

MEGA POWERS

WRITTEN BY
JACK WEYLAND!
ILLUSTRATED BY
KEN STEACY!

Wouldn't it be great to have x-ray vision? That way you could tell what was inside your birthday presents, what sort of sandwich your best friend brought for lunch and where your mother hid the left-over Hallowe'en candy.

X-rays are amazing things. They're cousins of the light you see coming from the sun or light bulbs. The difference is that x-rays have more energy than ordinary light. It's this higher energy that allows x-rays to zap through bodies, suitcases and even steel beams.

Suppose you were lucky enough to have x-ray vision (more about the chances of that happening later). Could you use your x-ray vision to detect a bomb in a box?

NOW YOU SEE IT...

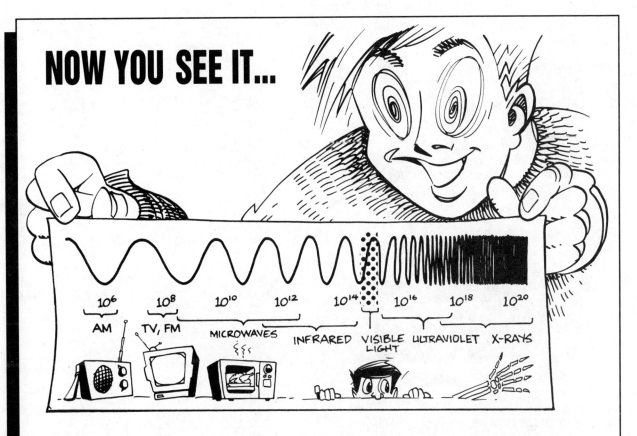

Our eyes are sensitive only to a small part of the light around us. The light we can see is called "the visible spectrum." But there are lots of other kinds of light that we aren't able to see. Light with a little more energy than visible light is called *ultraviolet light*. Light with a little less energy is called *infrared light*.

Other kinds of light we can't see are: gamma rays, x-rays, microwaves and radio and T.V. broadcasting signals. Wouldn't it be neat to see more of the light that's around us? You may be surprised to learn that we can. Astronomers have built telescopes with detectors sensitive to the infrared light coming from stars.

Infrared light is good for looking at old stars that are cooling down. Astronomers also use x-ray telescopes to look at supernovas (exploding stars).

Astronomers are discovering that the heavens look much different when we look through "eyes" that are sensitive to forms of light usually invisible to our eyes.

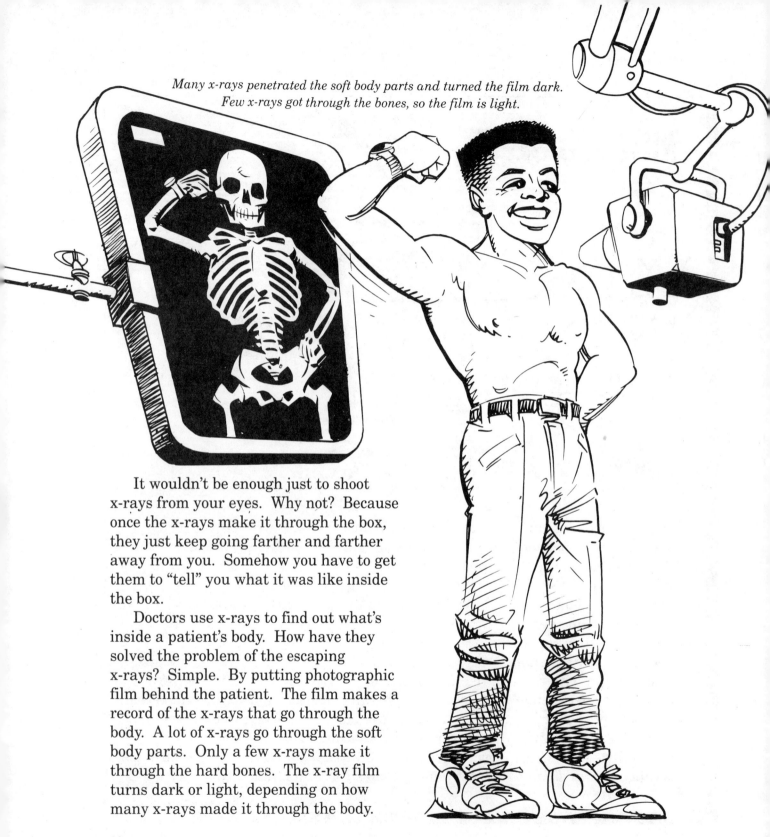

Many x-rays penetrated the soft body parts and turned the film dark.
Few x-rays got through the bones, so the film is light.

It wouldn't be enough just to shoot x-rays from your eyes. Why not? Because once the x-rays make it through the box, they just keep going farther and farther away from you. Somehow you have to get them to "tell" you what it was like inside the box.

Doctors use x-rays to find out what's inside a patient's body. How have they solved the problem of the escaping x-rays? Simple. By putting photographic film behind the patient. The film makes a record of the x-rays that go through the body. A lot of x-rays go through the soft body parts. Only a few x-rays make it through the hard bones. The x-ray film turns dark or light, depending on how many x-rays made it through the body.

When the doctor develops the film, she sees an outline of the person's bones. You can try a homemade "x-ray" and see for yourself.

You'll need:
• a dark room
• a flashlight

1. Turn off the lights.

2. Turn on the flashlight.

3. Place your fingers palm down over the light of the flashlight. Which parts of your fingers are lit up most? Which parts are dark? Can you locate blood vessels? (They will be dark lines.)

4. Try doing this on someone much younger than you and also on someone much older. Is there any difference? Why do you suppose that is?

Even though your "x-ray" is ordinary light and not the real x-rays, the effect is much the same. The light that has the easiest path to get through your fingers will show up as the brightest. You can see your flashlight "x ray" because your eyes are there to trap the light. If you had x-ray vision, your eyes would be sending out rays not catching them. So x-ray vision wouldn't work unless you used photographic film as a doctor does.

There's another little problem with x-ray vision. Your eyes aren't capable of sending out x-rays or any other kind of rays. They're *receivers* of light, not senders. Don't believe it? How much can you see in the dark?

A VISIT TO THE DOCTOR

Suppose you accidentally swallow a pocket dictionary one night while you're sleeping. You don't remember doing it, but the next morning your stomach doesn't feel very good. Also, you're starting to use words you've never known before, like umbilicus and mitochondrion. So you go to the doctor.

"Doctor," you say, "I fear I have a malady of cryptogenic origins."

The doctor looks worried. "I'll take an x-ray immediately."

The x-ray reveals a big rectangle. "From the shape," the doctor observes, "it could be a brick, a quart of ice cream, a book or a lunch bucket."

You feel worse.

"I'll tell you what. I'll take an x-ray from another angle."

A little later the doctor returns. "This time it looks like a small rectangle. It could be a book or it could be a quart of ice cream."

"Don't tell me what it could be. I want to know what it is."

"Okay, I'll take an x-ray from another angle." She looks at the new x-ray. "I think it's a book, and from the way you've been talking, my guess is that it's a dictionary."

Your doctor could have saved time by doing a CAT scan.

CAT stands for Computerized Axial Tomography. A thin beam of x-rays is sent through the body in various directions. Instead of the doctor taking multiple x-rays and guessing what they show, the CAT scan collects information from various positions and feeds it into a computer. The computer then creates an image that can be rotated and sends it to a T.V. screen. The outline of your pocket dictionary shows up on the screen.

So x-ray vision isn't going to help you find Gork's bomb after all. You stare at the three boxes. Then you notice a sand-filled dump truck rumbling down the street. You flag it down.

"Dump your sand on top of those boxes and then get out of here as fast as you can," you yell to the driver.

The boxes are no sooner buried in sand than the bomb goes off. The explosion only makes the sand jump a bit. The sand has absorbed the energy of the blast. Science has saved the day.

The driver of the truck comes back and hands you a shovel. "I'll be in the café across the street. Tell me when you've got all the sand back in my truck."

"I saved the city from certain destruction and you want me to clean up?" you ask.

He keeps on walking.

You throw the first shovelful of sand into the truck. It's going to be a long day.

YOU AND YOUR MEGAPOWERS: SIGHT

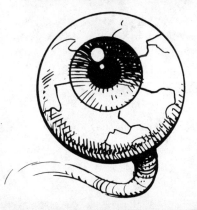

You've got two sets of sensors at the back of your eyes: 125 million rod cells for seeing in dim light and 7 million cone cells for sensing colours in bright light. Your eyes are so sensitive that, under ideal conditions, you could see the flame from a match on a mountain 80 km (50 miles) away.

The lens of the eye can be stretched or relaxed by the ciliary muscle. This allows you to see things either very far away or very close up.

For as long as people have watched birds soaring, they've dreamed about flying, so it's not surprising that most comic book megaheroes can fly. A megahero who has to wait for a bus would never get to the scene of an emergency in time to save the day.

But could a megahero take the place of a jet engine and fly a plane to safety? To do this, a megahero would have to work like a jet engine, right? So how do jet engines work?

Here's what a jet engine looks like inside.

Air is compressed and a mist of fuel is sprayed into it. Then the fuel and air mixture is set on fire, causing a backward rush of air out the back end of the jet.

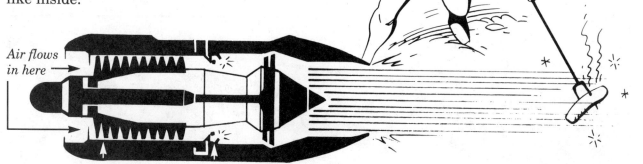

Air flows in here →

The air is compressed

Fuel is added and the mixture is set on fire

GODDARD 1, NEW YORK TIMES 0

In 1920, when rocket scientist Robert Goddard was developing a rocket to fly in outer space, an editorial in the *New York Times* criticized him, saying that a rocket wouldn't work in outer space because it had nothing to push against. (There's no air in outer space–there's nothing.)

The *New York Times* was wrong. Rockets today are used to send up the space shuttle, to make mid-course corrections and to return manned spacecraft from orbit.

BETTER THAN A RUBBER DUCKY

A private jet will cost you a million dollars. A speed boat will set you back twenty thousand dollars. If you don't have that kind of money to spend learning about jet propulsion, try this.

You'll need:
- an empty, flat-sided, waterproof container such as a baby-powder bottle
- a friendly adult with a knife
- a plastic straw
- a balloon
- a rubber band
- a clothespin

1. Have the adult cut the waterproof container in half lengthwise. You'll use one of the halves as your boat.

2. Get an adult to help you with this step. At the back of the boat near the bottom, cut a small hole not quite big enough for the straw to slide through.

3. Cut off a 7 cm (3 inch) section of straw. Place the neck of the balloon over the straw and hold it it there by twisting the rubber band over it several times.

4. Cram the other end of the straw through the hole in the back of the boat.

5. Blow up the balloon through the straw and clamp the clothespin over the neck of the balloon to keep the air from escaping. Set your boat in a bathtub containing water, remove the clothespin and watch the boat go!

How does this move the plane forward? Imagine that Gork has stranded you on a life raft in the middle of a pond. The pond is full of hungry crocodiles. You don't have a paddle but you do have a box of oranges with you.

Question: How can you get to shore?

A. Call out, "Hey, if someone will help get me to shore, I'll give them this box of very nice oranges."

B. Yell to a passing boat, "Want to trade some oranges for a paddle?"

C. Find out if crocodiles like oranges. If they do, quickly throw them out of the left side of the boat and swim to safety on the right side.

D. Use Newton's laws of motion.

The correct answer is D.

HOW DO YOU WALK?

Have you ever thought about how you walk? Stand up and take one slow-motion step. Can you feel yourself pushing backwards on the ground? It's Newton's law—you push backwards on the ground, so the ground pushes forwards on you. This forward force pushes you forwards.

How easy is it to walk on ice? You push back on the ice but your foot slips, so you're never able to push back as hard as you can on dry ground.

18

Isaac Newton was a scientist who studied motion and came up with laws to explain how things move. Newton's third law says: "If you push something, it will push back on you in the opposite direction with the same amount of force."

At first this sounds like something a crime boss would say. "Lean on me, Braxton, and I guarantee I'll lean on you back..." Except the mobster would add, "...ten times harder." Newton wasn't that vicious; he said the leaning back would be with exactly the same force.

SHUT UP, HORSE, AND PULL THE WAGON!

You hitch up a horse to a wagon and yell "Giddy up!" The horse turns around and says, "Excuse me, but if I can never pull any harder on the wagon than the wagon pulls back on me, how can I ever move the wagon?"

"Very clever, horse," you begin, "but not clever enough. You're right in saying that if you pull on the wagon, the wagon pulls back on you with the same force. But you forgot one thing. Every time you take a step you push back on the ground. According to Newton, if you push backwards on the ground, then the ground pushes forwards on you."

"So?"

"There are actually two forces acting on you. The force of the wagon acting backwards and the force of the ground in the forward direction. Whichever of these forces is greater will determine what direction you go."

"Oh, sure, I see now," the horse says. "But while we're at it, I have another question."

"What?"

"Why don't you get yourself a car like everyone else?"

So while the crocodiles are arguing about who has first dibs on you, you face the rear of the boat, pick up an orange and toss it as hard as you can. As you throw the orange, you push on it. According to Newton, the orange will push back on you with the same force, but in the opposite direction.

By tossing oranges out the back of the boat, you'll be pushed forwards. If you've got enough oranges, you'll make it to shore.

The same thing happens with jet and rocket engines. Air forced out the back of the jet engine pushes the engine (and the plane it's attached to) forwards.

A megahero would have to do the same thing to save the mayor's plane from crashing into the ground. But how? You could start by eating a megasized serving of beans.

How embarrassing for a megahero's mom. "Now dear, stop that!"

"But Mom, I'm saving the world from being destroyed."

"Don't give me that. I know what you're doing and it's rude. How many times have I told you to cut it out? No more beans for you."

"But, Mom..."

No one said it would be easy to be a megahero.

LOST IN SPACE ???

Suppose you were stranded in outer space away from your space vehicle with only a tank of compressed air. If you hold onto the tank and open the valve so the air comes out fast, what will happen? Try an Earth version of this experiment and find out.

You'll need:
• a water hose with a spray nozzle
• a skateboard
• heavy tape

1. Find a patch of smooth driveway within reach of your hose. Tape the hose to the skateboard.

2. Set the spray nozzle to send out a narrow jet of water.

3. Turn on the water and see if the skateboard is propelled backwards.

Wouldn't it be fun to be the strongest person in the world? Just think... you'd be able to bend a rifle barrel into a pretzel shape or lift a heavy weight. Throughout history, people have imagined heroes with superhuman strength –Superman, Darth Vader and the Teenage Mutant Ninja Turtles, to name a few.

How do megaheroes get to be so strong? Superman gets his strength because he was born on a planet where the force of gravity was much stronger than it is on Earth. His muscles had to be extra strong to deal with this high-gravity environment. On lower-gravity Earth, he seems to be inhumanly strong. Some megaheroes get their extra strength by using bionic limbs. Robocop was once a cop who was badly shot up trying to arrest a gang. Shortly after he was pronounced dead in a hospital, a team of doctors and computer experts began working on his body. They replaced his arms with bionic arms made out of extra strong titanium. Presto–he had incredible strength.

YOU AND YOUR MEGAPOWERS: BONES

The skeleton of your body is like the steel framework of a sky-scraper. The more than 200 bones in your skeleton can hold up a body five times their own weight.

Even more amazing, your thigh-bone is stronger pound for pound than reinforced concrete.

Less force but more distance

More force but less distance

Having superhuman strength sounds great, but would it be? Suppose you had bionic arms. You're walking down the street when all of a sudden a car comes around a corner and heads towards you. Gork is at the wheel laughing as he tries to run you down. When the car gets to you, you grab it and fling it into space. You can do that because you have bionic arms, right?

Wrong. It won't do much good to have extra strong arms unless you also had an extra strong spine, because any force you exert in pushing or pulling eventually makes its way to your back. Even the strongest of heroes would have a bad back if he or she wasn't careful lifting things.

You may not have superhuman strength, but don't let that stop you. You can do most of the things megaheroes do. How? With the help of some simple machines.

Suppose you wanted to lift a 250 kg (500 pound) carrot off the ground. (If you think that's big, you should see the rabbit.) You could just grab the carrot and try lifting it, but unless you're Superman, you're not going to even budge it.

If you could find a long ramp that sloped gradually upward, you could push the carrot up the ramp. But there's both good news and bad news about the ramp idea. The good news is that the more gradual the slope, the easier it is to push the carrot up the ramp. The bad news is that the more gradual the slope, the greater the distance you have to push the carrot in order to get it off the ground. So what you save in force, you make up for in distance. As someone once said, there's no free lunch, not even if that lunch is an enormous carrot.

But hey, look, there's a tree right next to the carrot. If you tie a rope around the carrot and loop it over a tree branch and pull, you might be in luck. That way, instead of pulling up to lift the carrot, you can pull down and let your weight help you with the lifting. You are using the tree branch as a pulley. (A pulley is just a device that changes the direction of the pull on a rope.)

So you try it. Groan, sweat, grunt....Nope. No matter how hard you pull, the carrot won't budge.

So far the tree hasn't done you much good. But suppose nine of your friends come with ropes to help out. If all ten of you tie the end of your ropes to the carrot and loop the other ends over the tree branch, and if you all pull at the same time, then each one of you will have to pull only one-tenth of the weight. Each of you has to lift only 25 kg (50 pounds) of the rabbit food.

But what if your friends won't help? It would be just like them, right? You can replace them with a set of pulleys. If the rope is looped back and forth ten times and you pull on it with a force enough to lift 25 kg (50 pounds), the resulting pull is as strong as if you and nine friends were pulling ten ropes. So the total force being exerted is equal to 25 kg (50 pounds) x 10, or 250 kg (500 pounds). Your friends have been replaced by a set of pulleys. Don't tell them though; it might hurt their feelings. Besides, who wants to go to a movie with a pulley?

A system of pulleys that makes it easier to lift heavy objects is called a block and tackle. With a block and tackle you can lift weights that would challenge even Superman.

MAKE A BLOCK AND TACKLE

The roller that toilet paper fits onto can be used to make a block and tackle.

You'll need:
- scissors
- string
- an empty spool of thread
- an empty toilet paper dispenser still fastened to the wall
- a plastic shopping bag
- a can of soup

1. Cut a 45 cm (18 inch) length of string and slide it through the spool of thread.

2. Tie a 2.5 cm (1 inch) loop on each end of the string. Slide these loops onto the roller of the toilet paper dispenser.

3. Cut another 45 cm (18 inch) length of string and slide it, too, through the spool of thread.

Tie the ends to the handles of the plastic shopping bag.

4. Place a can of soup in the shopping bag.

5. Cut a 2 m (6 foot) length of string. Tie a 2.5 cm (1 inch) loop on one end. Remove one of the loops connecting the spool of thread to the toilet paper roller, slide the loop you've just made into the middle of the roller and slide the loop you've removed back on again.

6. Wind this string around the spool of thread, up and over the toilet paper roller. Repeat this four or five times. Every time you complete one loop, you'll make it easier to lift the can of soup. Try to keep the looped sections bunched closely together in the centre of the spool.

7. Slowly pull on the free end of the string What happens?

8. Try looping the string over the roll just once and pull the can of soup up. Can you tell the difference? What happens if you loop the string over twice? What about four, five or six times?

The next time you see a crane at a building site, count the number of times the cable is looped over the rollers.

MAY THE TORQUE BE WITH YOU

If you push on a door right next to the hinges, you have to push hard to get the door to move, but if you push far away from the hinges, where the doorknob is, for instance, it's easy. In this case, the hinges are the pivot point. If the force is applied close to the hinges, you need a large force, but if it's far from the hinges, you can open the door with a much smaller force.

Science has a name for the combination of force and distance that makes things rotate. It's called *torque* and it rhymes with fork.

The next time someone says, "That torques me off," you'll know what they mean.

Suppose you don't have a block and tackle. How else can you lift that troublesome carrot? Why not try a lever?

A lever is just a teeter-totter that's escaped the playground. To turn a board into a lever, you first need a pivot point. That's something that will support the weight of the board and allow it to teeter (or totter). To make the best use of a lever, you need to be very clever about where you put the pivot point. When you're on a teeter-totter with someone much heavier than you, your friend has to move towards the centre support in order to balance your different weights. (You could also move the centre support towards your heavier friend.) Where you put the pivot point makes a big difference. See for yourself.

You'll need:
- a chair with a back rest about the same height as one of the light switches in your house. Put the chair on some books if it's not high enough.
- a wooden metre (yard) stick

1. Put the chair about one large step away from a wall where there's a light switch. The chair should have its back to the wall.

2. Try to turn on the light with the measuring stick by resting the measuring stick on the back of the chair and pushing down on one end. Be careful not to break the measuring stick as you push down.

3. Move the chair a little closer to the wall so that the chair back is in the middle of the measuring stick. Keep moving the chair closer to the wall until you can turn the light on easily.

The back of the chair acts as the pivot point. Where you put the pivot point can make it easy or hard to turn on the light, just as where your friend sits on the teeter-totter makes it easy or difficult to lift him or her.

How do you lift a 250 kg (500 pound) carrot with a lever? Place a rock close to the carrot, set a board on the rock, tip the end of the board to the ground and then roll the carrot onto the board. While a friend keeps the carrot from falling off the board, go to the other end of the board and, using the rock as the pivot point, push down. You won't have to push very hard to lift the carrot.

Ramps, pulleys, block and tackles, and levers can make even a 98-pound weakling look like Superman. And they just might help you foil Gork so you can get the key to the locker containing the poison gas out from under the weight.

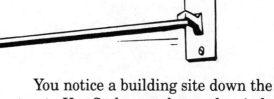

You notice a building site down the street. You find a crowbar and a cinder block there and carry them to the weight under which Gork has hidden the key.

Using the cinder block as a pivot point, you pry up the weight with the crow bar. There's the key just as Gork promised. Key in hand, you head for the coliseum. Minutes later, you grab the container of poisonous gas in the locker and turn off the timer before it can explode.

Gork watches as you leave the coliseum. "You want to know something?" he asks. "You really torque me off."

"Precisely," you say with a smile.

YOU HEAR GORK COMING CLOSER... THERE *MUST* BE SOMETHING YOU CAN DO, BUT *WHAT?*

BUT *WAIT,* EVEN THOUGH YOUR MEGASTRENGTH IS GONE, YOU STILL HAVE YOUR POWER OF *INVISIBILITY!*

A SECOND LATER GORK FLINGS THE DOOR OPEN, BUT ALL HE SEES IS AN *EMPTY* ROOM!

I KNOW YOU'RE IN HERE!

HE MISSES YOU BY A MILE! YOU GRAB HIS PISTOL, SLIP OUT THE DOOR AND LOCK IT BEHIND YOU!

I'LL GET YOU NEXT TIME!

What would you do if you could become invisible? Find out what people say about you when they think you're not around? Visit friends whenever you want, even when their parents say it's too late? Scare people by making strange sounds or by moving objects around? Go into the kitchen and sneak an extra piece of cake?

Being invisible would be great, but is it possible?

Suppose your brother is watching T.V. and you stand in front of it. He'll probably yell at you to move. Why? Because your body is blocking the picture, making it impossible for him to see the show he's watching. You'll be invisible only if the T.V. picture seen by your brother is the same as if you weren't there.

Basically there are two ways for you to become invisible: either light can go through your body and out again or you can use something to detour the light around your body.

Getting light to pass through your body isn't so easy. It's not just a matter of smearing an invisible lotion on your skin. Even if your skin disappeared, your skeleton, liver, lungs, heart and other organs would still block the light.

If you somehow managed to make all your body parts invisible, you'd be in for a nasty surprise. People wouldn't see you, but neither could you see them. Why not? In order to see things, a lens in your eye must form an image on the back of your eye. It's a bit like a movie being projected on a screen. You need the screen to see the picture. The same thing happens in your eye. If the screen is invisible, you couldn't see any image. You'd not only be invisible–you'd be blind.

What about the other alternative–detouring the light around you? Is it possible to get light to hang a left? Try this and see.

You'll need:
- a hammer and a nail and an adult to supervise
- an empty metal coffee can
- a dark room with a sink
- a flashlight

1. Use the hammer and nail to make a hole on the side of the coffee can near the bottom.

2. Set the can on the counter by a sink or else do the experiment outside.

3. Plug the hole in the can with your thumb and fill the can with water.

4. Turn off the room lights and shine the flashlight into the water towards the bottom of the can. **(DON'T let the flashlight touch the water.)** Remove your thumb so that the water can flow out of the hole.

Notice anything strange about the water coming out of the hole? Put your hand into the stream of water and see your hand light up. The light is pouring out of the can along with the water!

You've found a way to make light bend. You could also have used a light-pipe. A light-pipe is a long, thin filament made out of transparent materials such as glass

DON'T let the flashlight touch the water

or plastic (or, as you just found out, even water). Once light gets into a light-pipe, it bounces from side to side until it reaches the end. If the light-pipe bends, so does the light inside it. This is a great benefit because usually light only travels in a straight line. Light-pipes are used in fibre optics phone systems.

To appear to be invisible, you'd need a lot of tiny light-pipes to detour light around you. Let's say you're facing your brother in front of the T.V. The light comes from the T.V., enters a light-pipe, takes the detour around your body, gets to the end of the light-pipe and proceeds on its way to your brother. When he looks at the T.V., your brother sees the picture as if you weren't there. You're invisible! Go ahead and make faces at him! But don't move or he'll see you and ask, "How come you've got all those plastic tubes around you?"

Unfortunately, even if you had a thousand fibres from your front to your back, you probably wouldn't be able to capture every bit of the T.V. picture, so your brother could tell it wasn't the same. If you moved even a tiny bit, the T.V. picture would move, too. That would be a dead giveaway. Also, anyone else coming into the room would be able to see you.

You can't really make yourself invisible as in the movies, but you can come close to it by using some simple science. Try the optical trick of blending into the background. It works for many animals. The twig caterpillar looks like a twig on a tree. It doesn't move all day. Hungry birds don't even notice it because it has brown skin that is bumpy like a real twig. When night falls, the caterpillar moves around and eats leaves from the tree it calls home.

In nature there are caterpillars that look like leaves or bird droppings, insects that look like stones and moths that look like broken wood. Blending in with the background to become invisible or at least less visible is called "camouflage."

ARE YOU STRONG ENOUGH TO BEND LIGHT?

Each of your eyes has a lens to focus the light entering it. What is a lens and how does it work?

You'll need:
- scissors
- a piece of poster paper or a recipe card
- a flashlight
- a sheet of white paper
- pair of prescription eyeglasses

1. Cut out slots in the poster paper as shown.

2. Hold the slotted paper against the flashlight.

3. Place the white paper on a table in front of the slotted paper.

4. Turn on the flashlight. As the light goes through the slots, it will produce bright and dark patches on the white paper. Sketch on the paper the patches of light or darkness.

5. Place one lens of the eyeglasses in front of the slotted paper. Does the pattern of bright and dark patches change? What does the lens do? Does it bend the light out or bend it in?

Some eyeglasses bend light inward while others bend it out. Why? Images are supposed to form on the back of your eyes so that light-sensitive nerve cells can detect the image and send the information to your brain. If the lens in your eye is too strong, the light focuses in front of where it should. When this happens, people say you're nearsighted. You need an extra eyeglass lens to spread the light out before it gets to your eye. The lens in your eye and the lens on your glasses work together to focus the light where it's supposed to be. If the lens in your eye isn't strong enough, the image will be behind where it should be. You're said to be far-sighted. You need a lens that bends the light inward.

There's another kind of camouflage used by both nature and soldiers. Instead of blending in, you use a pattern of colours to break up your outline. If you're looking for the outline of a person in the woods, but instead see patches of colour of various shades of browns and greens, you probably won't recognize them as being on a person.

Some tropical fish have bold vertical and horizontal stripes. At first you think the fish might as well have a sign on its back that says, "Hungry? Try me. I'm tasty." But against the brightly coloured coral, the fish's outline is broken up; it doesn't look like a fish.

Camouflage is mostly used by animals that want to avoid being eaten. But some animal hunters use camouflage, too. Tigers need camouflage because other animals have learned not to trust them. (It has something to do with the fact the other animals keep getting eaten.) The stripes on a tiger do two things. They blend in with the long grass where the tiger hides, and they break up the tiger's body shape so that it's harder to recognize.

How are people made to look invisible in movies? The first movie with this theme was *The Invisible Man*, starring Claude Rains, made in 1933. In one scene, Claude Rains, his face totally wrapped in bandages, takes off his glasses, bandages and gloves. As he unwraps the bandages, there's no head. He's completely invisible!

To do that scene, a stuntman put on a black velvet body suit, including a black velvet mask and gloves. Then he put on his normal clothing. When the scene was filmed, the stuntman stood in front of a backdrop also made of black velvet. When he took off his hat and bandages, the black of his mask blended in with the black background. To the audience he looked invisible.

How would you like to be the first in your neighbourhood to become invisible? Try this some dark night.

You'll need:
- scissors
- 2 m (6 feet) of black felt or any material that is cheap but not shiny
- a chair
- rubber bands
- a pair of brightly coloured mittens
- a Hallowe'en mask
- a friend to help

1. Cut the black material in half. One half will be for your head and hands; the other half will go on the wall behind you. Hang one piece of the black material on the wall right behind a chair. When you sit on the chair, the black cloth should be behind your upper body.

2. From the rest of the black cloth, cut out a large circle. This is to cover your head. Cut out two smaller circles. These are for over your hands.

3. Have someone wrap the small circles over your hands and fasten them with rubber bands. Put a pair of mittens on over the black material.

4. Have someone drape the large circle over your head and neck. Make sure it's loose enough so you can breathe. You might want to cut a hole in the back of the mask to let in more air. Take the mask off before cutting. Put the mask back on when you're done. Pull a sweater over your head and tuck the black material inside the neck hole. Put on the Hallowe'en mask.

5. Get your friend to arrange the room so that the lighting is very dim. He or she might have to experiment to get the lighting right. Sit on the chair in front of the black background. Invite an unsuspecting friend or family member to enter the room. When someone comes into the room, say something like this. "Excuse me for wearing this mask, but you'll soon see why. Last night I was at the university. One of the professors was working on a strange liquid. When he stepped out of the room to answer a phone, I drank some of the liquid. Since then, odd things have been happening to me. Here, you can see for yourself." Now take off the Hallowe'en mask and remove the mittens. Have your helper gasp and cry out that you're invisible.

STARBUCK IS SO HAPPY TO SEE YOU THAT HE WAGS HIS TAIL...DESTROYING THREE BUILDINGS AND A TOUR BUS FROM HOBOKEN!

STOP HIM!

SIT, STARBUCK, SIT!

STARBUCK SITS—ON THE STATEN ISLAND FERRY TERMINAL BUILDING!

TAKE HIM TO NEW JERSEY! THEY WON'T NOTICE!

SUDDENLY, YOUR WORST NIGHTMARE COMES TO PASS! STARBUCK SEES A RED WATER TOWER THAT LOOKS LIKE A FIRE HYDRANT!

NO, STARBUCK, NO!

SECONDS LATER, YOU, THE MAYOR AND 5000 OTHER PEOPLE ARE FLOATING DOWNTOWN! IT LOOKS LIKE GORK HAS WON THIS TIME!

You say you don't like spiders? Imagine battling one twice your size. For many of us our worst nightmare is to be small compared to some gigantic creature that wants to step on us. Maybe it's because we all started out as babies surrounded by giants called adults.

In movies there are two ways to be small. The world remains the same while you become so small that the simplest things seem huge. Or you stay your normal size and everything else becomes much larger.

Every so often you'll hear about some gardener who's grown a 90 kg (200 pound) pumpkin. So maybe it is possible for some creatures to get super big. After all there used to be some very large creatures. Dinosaurs were big, mammoths were big. So why not huge cats, bats and dogs? To find out, try this.

You'll need:
- a ruler
- a pencil
- cardboard that can be cut with a pair of scissors
- scissors
- rubber bands or some string or sticky tape
- three plastic bags
- three plates
- your favourite pudding, already made
- a teaspoon

1. With a ruler and a pencil draw a 2.5 cm (1 inch) square on the cardboard.

2. Draw identical 2.5 cm (1 inch) squares on top of, below and to each side of your original square as shown.

3. Do the same thing with 5 cm (2 inch) squares.

4. Do the same thing with 8 cm (3 inch) squares.

5. Cut out the cross-like shapes.

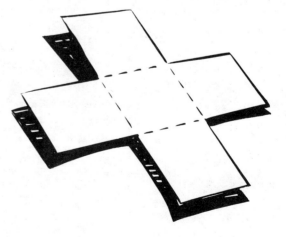

6. For each one, fold up the outer squares to make a box.

7. Fasten rubber bands around the sides of each box to keep the box from falling apart. Or use sticky tape or string.

8. Line the inside of each box with a piece of plastic bag.

9. Place each box on a plate, just in case things get messy. Start with the smallest box and put the pudding in one spoonful at a time. How many spoonfuls does it take to fill the box to the top?

10. Do the same for the other boxes. Count the number of spoonfuls of pudding it takes to fill each box.

The medium box was twice as big as the small box. Did it take twice as much pudding to fill it, or did it take more than that? How much more? Four times, 8 times, 16 times? What about the large box? How much more did it take to fill it compared to the medium box? Is it 3 times, 9 times, 18 times, 27 times?

When the length of one side of a square box doubles, its volume increases more than just twice. So does the weight. If Gork were able to make Starbuck 100 times bigger than normal, the dog would weigh about a million times more than normal. Unfortunately Starbuck's bones, even though they would be 100 times thicker, wouldn't be strong enough to support all that extra weight. When he took a step, his legs would snap in two and he'd fall down. The dinosaurs were luckier. Their bones were extra thick to support their weight.

What if Gork shrunk you so that Starbuck *looked* big? Besides the fact that you'd be the last to be chosen for the volleyball team, what other problems would you have? Try this and find out.

You'll need:
- a potato peeler
- 1 very large potato that weighs about 0.5 kg (1 pound)
- several very small potatoes with a total weight of about 0.5 kg (1 pound)

1. Peel the large potato first. Put the peelings in one pile.

2. Peel the small potatoes next. Put the peelings in another pile. Which pile has the most peelings?

The amount of peelings is a measure of something called surface area. The small potatoes have more peelings and therefore more surface area than the large potato.

BE SURFACE AREA SMART

Why is it better to crush ice than to use ice cubes when you want to cool your drink as quickly as possible? With the smaller bits of ice, your drink comes in contact with more ice surface area and cools faster.

When you want to start a bonfire, why do you use small sticks and twigs instead of a big log? Again, to increase the surface area where wood burns.

What cools faster? Soup in a large, flat dish or in a tall mug? Hint: which container exposes more of the soup's surface area to the air?

All small things have more surface area, for their size, than large things. If you were shrunk, the same would be true of you. You'd have more surface area for your size than you have now. And that would spell trouble.

First, you'd be hungry all the time. You'd need to eat about twenty meals a day. Why? A creature loses heat through the surface of its body. A small creature that has a large surface area for its size loses a lot more heat for its size. To replace that heat, it has to eat all the time or die.

Another problem—if you were the size of a fly, you'd also have a brain the size of a fly's, so you wouldn't be thinking much about any of this at all.

Although giant monsters and tiny shrunken people really couldn't exist in our world, science fiction movies create fantasies about them. How do they do it? Surprisingly, to film huge creatures like King Kong, miniature models are used. In a 1933 version of the movie *King Kong,* the big ape star was a 45 cm (18 inch) model covered in dyed rabbit fur. This mini-monster towered over an even smaller model of a city. For scenes showing actress Fay Wray being held by King Kong, a large mechanical hand, large enough for Wray to sit in, was constructed.

By the way, when you think of giant monsters, you might just think about yourself. If you write down all the animals that are larger than humans, your list could easily take up a page. But if you list all the animals smaller than humans, it'd take hundreds of pages. The next time you take a walk, think of all the creatures who fear you because to them you're a giant.

Maybe you and King Kong have something in common after all.

IS THERE ANYONE DOWN THERE?!

Help!

YOU LOWER THE BUCKET DOWN INTO THE WELL, AND AS YOU PULL, OUT COMES A YOUNG KID!

THANKS!

WHO DID THIS TO YOU?

A MAN NAMED GORK, HE WANTED YOU TO KNOW THAT WHILE YOU'VE BEEN SAVING ME HE'S BEEN ROBBING A BANK!

YOU SPEED TO THE POLICE STATION AND TELL THEM ABOUT GORK'S SCHEME! POLICE SIRENS WAIL AS YOU HEAD BACK TO SCHOOL.

Wouldn't it be handy to hear things happening far away? Suppose you are watching T.V. late at night. When you hear your parents' car turning the corner onto your street, you quickly shut off the television and hop into bed.

Megahearing sounds like fun, but is it possible? How good is normal hearing, anyway? Suppose two of your friends are talking to each other. How far away from them can you be and still hear what they're saying? See for yourself.

You'll need:
- 2 friends (2 enemies will also work)
- a couple of small rocks to use as markers
- a measuring tape

1. Have your two friends stand side by side and carry on a normal conversation. (It's not necessary for the experiment, but tell them it says in the book they're supposed to talk about how wonderful you are.)

2. Start walking away from them until you can't make out what they're saying. Mark where you're standing with a rock, then measure the distance from you to your friends.

3. Now tell your friends to whisper as softly as they can. How far away can you get from them when they're whispering before you can no longer make out what they're saying? Mark the spot and measure the distance.

4. Get your friends to yell and try measuring again.

YOU AND YOUR MEGAPOWERS: HEARING

You can hear the rustle of leaves or the roar of a jet engine and everything in between. You can also tell where a sound is coming from. How do you do it? Try this and find out.

You'll need:
• a curious friend
• a scarf

1. Blindfold your friend with a scarf. Snap your fingers to one side of his head. Ask him to point to where the sound is coming from. Try finger snapping at various places around his head. Can he tell where the sound is coming from?

2. Now snap your fingers behind his head the same distance from either ear. Can he tell where the sound is coming from?

Usually, sound reaches one ear before the other. This acts as a signal to your brain: "The sound is over there." But you've made sure your friend hears the sound at the same time in both ears. Because of this, he won't be able to tell where the sound is coming from. His brain will be confused.

The farther you get away from a sound, the harder it is to hear it. You probably already know this...but why is it so? Find out for yourself.

You'll need:

- 3 pennies
- a pond or wading pool or a bathtub half full of water
- small wood chips or corks

1. Drop one penny into the water. Notice how a wave moves out in circles.

2. Place a wood chip or cork on the water and drop the penny about 15 cm (6 inches) away. Watch how high the wood chip bobs when the wave passes by.

3. Wait till the surface of the water is smooth. Now drop a penny about 1 metre (3 feet) from the wood chip. How high does the wood chip bob this time?

There's only so much energy in the circular wave you've made. As the wave moves outward, that energy has to be shared by a larger and larger circle. This means there's less energy at any one point in the circle to lift the wood chip. (It's a bit like having to share a chocolate bar among an increasing number of friends. Everyone gets less.)

Like the waves in water, as sound waves move through air, their energy has to be shared. When sound energy is very low, other noises may hide the sound. For example, the rustling of the leaves on a tree or the sound of someone mowing a lawn across the street would mask the cries for help from the kid in the well. Even with megahearing, you still wouldn't be able to make out what you were hearing. And the evil Gork would triumph again.

But don't get discouraged. With the help of science you can hear someone speaking on the other side of the world just by turning on a radio or T.V. or dialing someone's phone number. All of these turn sound into an electrical signal, send the electrical signal and then turn the electrical signal back into sound.

Ever wonder how a phone works?
Here's your chance to find out.

You'll need:
- an adult who likes to find out how things work and will be there as you dismantle his/her phone
- a telephone

1. Unplug the phone from the wall while you're working on it. Unscrew the part of the phone you talk into. You'll see a round disc. This disc converts your voice into an electrical signal that can be transmitted anywhere around the world.

2. Replace the cover of the mouthpiece. Unscrew the other part of the phone receiver. You'll see another disc; this one has two wires connected to the back. This part of the phone can turn the electrical signal back into a voice you can recognize.

How is it possible to turn a voice into an electrical signal? One way is to use a small round box filled with powdered carbon with a flexible front called a diaphragm. Clap your hands near the box and the diaphragm will be pushed in by the pressure from the clap. That will pack the particles of powdered carbon closer together. If electricity is forced through the powdered carbon, it flows through more easily when the carbon is packed tighter together. So there's more electrical current. Between hand claps the carbon spreads out again and there's less electrical current.

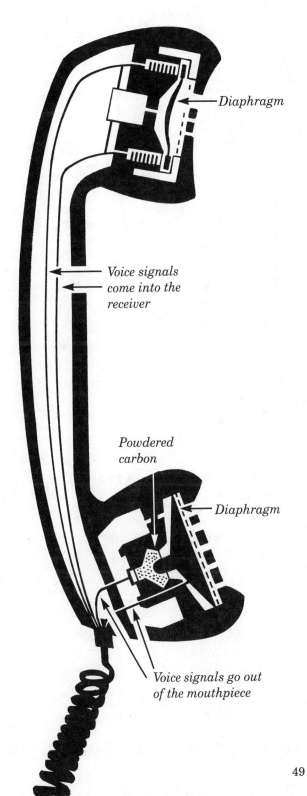

Diaphragm

Voice signals come into the receiver

Powdered carbon

Diaphragm

Voice signals go out of the mouthpiece

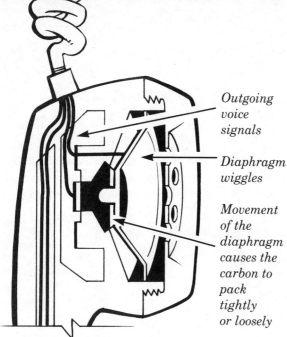

Outgoing voice signals

Diaphragm wiggles

Movement of the diaphragm causes the carbon to pack tightly or loosely

The same thing happens when you talk into the phone. The diaphragm wiggles back and forth, causing the electrical signal to vary. These wiggles in the electrical current give a record of what you're saying. That signal can be sent all over the world.

How can your friend on another phone know what you're saying? First, the electrical signals must be changed back into sound.

The part of the phone your friend listens to has many turns of wire wrapped around the outside of a disc. This coil of wire is really a small electromagnet. The more electricity that goes through the coil of wire, the stronger a magnet it becomes.

Just in front of the electromagnet is a thin piece of iron. If you yelled into the phone, you would produce a large electrical current, which flows through the electromagnet making it a strong magnet that attracts iron. So the wiggling signal makes the magnet either strong or weak, which, in turn, makes the piece of metal in front of the magnet wiggle, too. This causes the air to wiggle, making sound.

MAY THE SOUND BE WITH YOU

What if you were stranded away from your spaceship in outer space and all you had was a violin. You could play the violin to signal to your comrades in the mother ship. Right? Wrong. Playing your violin won't help you. Why not?

A. If your comrades hate violin music, they might decide to leave you.

B. If you play the violin badly, they *will* leave you.

C. There's no sound in outer space.

The correct answer is C.

Without any air molecules to be bumped around, there can be no sound. Watch for this mistake the next time you watch *Star Wars*.

YOU HEARD IT HERE FIRST

Imagine if you went to a rock concert and got stuck way at the back of the auditorium. Your brother, at camp 160 km (100 miles) away, turns on the radio to catch the concert live. Which of you hears the concert first?

As amazing as it seems, your brother might hear it first. Sound travels about 335 m (1100 feet) a second but radio waves travel 300 000 km (186 000 miles) a second. In the time it takes sound to travel 46 m (150 feet), a radio wave can travel around the world!

The next time you're talking on the phone, remember you're not really hearing your friend's voice. You're hearing "voice-like" sounds made from electrical signals.

Science has come up with another way to improve your hearing. Suppose Gork was meeting with some of the biggest crime bosses in the country. How could you listen in? By using a "bug." An electronic bug is like a miniature radio station that can allow you to hear what Gork is talking about in his secret meeting.

Bugs have become more and more elaborate recently. For instance, imagine that Gork and a crime boss are having a conversation in a hotel room. As they talk, they produce sound waves, which travel through the room. Some of those sound waves strike the window, causing the glass to wiggle ever so slightly. To listen in on their conversation, you could shine a laser beam at the window and capture the wiggling reflection of the laser beam. Then you could convert those wiggles back into sound.

With so many ways to turn sound into electrical signals, who needs megahearing? Besides, maybe megahearing would be more of a curse than a blessing. Say you were at a hockey game with 20 000 other fans. Who'd want to hear 4 000 people cough in unison, 3 000 belch and 7 000 chew nachos at the same time?

JUST THEN THE PRINCIPAL CALLS YOU TO HER OFFICE, YOU FIND YOURSELF FACING A VERY STERN *GOVERNMENT AGENT!*

WE NEED YOUR HELP, GORK HAS *KIDNAPPED* THE PRESIDENT OF FRANCE, THERE'S NO TIME TO SEND YOU BY PLANE, BUT WE'VE JUST DEVELOPED A BEAMING DEVICE LIKE THE ONE ON *STAR TREK*, WE'VE TRIED IT OUT HUNDREDS OF TIMES ON *MICE...*

LET ME GET THIS *STRAIGHT*-YOU'VE *NEVER* TRIED TO BEAM A PERSON BEFORE?!

WELL *NO*, BUT IT'S GONE VERY *SMOOTHLY* WITH MICE.

AND THE MICE WOULD HAVE *TOLD* YOU IF THERE WAS A PROBLEM, *RIGHT?*

THE GOVERNMENT AGENT *DOESN'T* SMILE. MOMENTS LATER YOU STEP INTO THE BEAMING CHAMBER, WONDERING IF THE MICE WERE AS WORRIED AS YOU ARE!

Who hasn't envied Captain Kirk of "Star Trek?" When he was in a sticky situation, all he had to do was issue the order, "Beam me up, Scotty," and he'd be instantly transported back to the safety of the starship *Enterprise*. Beaming up would certainly make life easier. No more sitting in the back seat of the car on long trips listening to your parents tell you what it was like when they were growing up.

The idea behind beaming up is simple enough. Suppose you have a set of coloured building blocks and a friend has exactly the same set. You build a castle from your building blocks, then phone your friend and explain to him where each coloured block is located. Because of the information you supply and the fact that he has the same building blocks, your friend can construct an exact duplicate of your castle.

Beaming up works much the same way–in theory. Suppose you could step in front of some kind of analyzer that could determine the position and type of every molecule in your body. If that information were telephoned or radioed to a friend who has a supply of various kinds of molecules, your friend or a special machine could theoretically create another you.

It sounds possible until you realize that you contain a billion billion billion molecules. Not only that–your friend needs to know the exact position and speed of every single molecule. At the rate of a million bits of information a second, it would take millions of years to send all that is needed to create another you.

When it was received, your friend would still have to assemble all those molecules in the right order. That would also take millions of years.

Even if you discovered how to beam, problems could arise. What if you were beaming a friend to your house and the power went out?

Your sister comes into your room. "What's that?"

"That's half my friend."

Her mouth drops open. "Where's the other half?"

"I'm not exactly sure."

"I'm telling."

You hope the power comes back on before your mother gets to your room. Things like this are hard to explain.

YOU CAN COUNT ON IT!

Would you rather be a millionaire or a billionaire? How big a number is a billion, anyway? Here's your chance to find out.

You'll need:
• a watch that can count seconds

1. Time yourself as you count to 100. It would take ten times as long to count to 1000 because there are ten 100s in 1000.

2. A million is a thousand 1000s. How long would it take to count to one million?

3. A billion is a thousand million. How long would it take to count to one billion?

4. How about a billion-billion? (Multiply the time for one billion by a billion.)

5. The number of molecules in your body is about one billion billion billion. How long would it take to count to that number? Now you can see why beaming up isn't such a good idea.

So much for instant travel. But wouldn't it be fun to fool your friends into thinking you know how to beam something across space? Try this.

You'll need:
- 2 aces of hearts from two identical decks of cards
- glue
- a loaf of bread

1. Set the two cards on top of each other and tear identical corners from both at the same time.

2. Use a tiny bit of glue and glue one of the cards back together again. After the glue is dry, return it to the deck of cards.

3. Place the larger piece of the other card between slices in a loaf of bread.

4. Tell a friend you've learned how to beam objects from one place to another. Pull the card from the deck and tear it along where it was glued. Place the small piece of the card on the table in front of your friend.

5. Hide the large piece of the card in your hand as you pretend to put it in the beaming machine, the freezing compartment of your refrigerator. Get rid of it as you walk back and forth explaining how the beaming machine works.

6. Tell your friend you've beamed the card into the loaf of bread. Let your friend sort through the loaf and find the card. "Prove" it's the right piece by taking the small piece of card and showing that it fits the card you've beamed.

How long does it take your friend to figure out what you've done?

You can't be beamed around like Captain Kirk, but there are other ways to travel instantly. For instance, want to visit the planet Venus? Think twice before you answer. The temperature on Venus is so hot you'd fry in a second and there's no air to breathe—only carbon dioxide at about 90 times Earth's atmospheric pressure. Not a nice place to visit, but don't let that stop you. You can travel instantly to Venus thanks to that miracle of modern technology, television pictures. In 1982 a Soviet spacecraft landed on Venus and beamed back pictures for the world to see—until the heat finally got to it and it signed off forever.

Television is one way that everyone from rock stars to escaped prisoners can be beamed into your living room instantly. But television is only two dimensional. If a rock star is beamed into your living room, you can't see what's printed on the back of his t-shirt by walking around the back of the T.V. Holograms, on the other hand, are three dimensional. (Some credit cards have holograms on them.) If a rock star arrived by hologram at your house, he'd look real. But try to hug him and you'd soon know the difference. It would be like hugging air.

WE'VE LEARNED *NOT* TO TELL MANY JOKES AROUND HIM!

LET'S GET THIS OVER WITH, JOE!

A SINISTER *SMILE* FORMS ON SERIOUS JOE'S LIPS... YOU WONDER IF THE *FORCE BUBBLE* YOU'VE JUST INVENTED WILL *WORK!*

WHEN THE BULLETS HIT THE FORCE BUBBLE, THEY BOUNCE OFF, LEAVING YOU *SAFE* AND *PROTECTED!*

NOW IT'S *MY* TURN TO SMILE!

EXIT

Wouldn't it be great to walk down the street with an invisible force shield around you? If a mugger tried to grab you, his arms would be stopped by your force bubble. Even if he pulled out a gun and shot at you, the bullet would just bounce off the bubble.

Force bubbles work well in comics, but what about in real life? Here in the real world, there are only four basic forces: the force of **gravity**, two kinds of **nuclear** forces and **electromagnetic** force. Those are the only forces you'd have to work with if you wanted to invent a force bubble.

You may be surprised to discover that gravitational force is the weakest of the four forces. Of course, when you fall from a tree, you might not think it's very weak. But the force responsible for making you tumble is the gravitational attraction of the entire planet Earth for you. Because the Earth is so big, its gravitational force is large enough to pull you to the ground very quickly. But the force of gravity you exert on a friend sitting next to you is less than one millionth of a pound.

If you're going to build a force bubble to protect yourself, forget about using gravity. The gravitational force is far too small to repel bullets or anything else. Also, the gravitational force always attracts; it never repels. You don't want your force shield *attracting* bullets, do you?

THE ANTI-GRAVITY TRICK

Wouldn't it be fun to fool your friends into believing you've discovered an anti-gravity machine? To prove it, you can show them a picture of you floating above your bed!

You'll need:
- permission from a parent to rearrange a bedroom and two adults to help
- a sheet of white paper or cardboard
- a drinking glass
- scissors
- sticky tape
- a wall poster
- duct tape
- a camera with film

1. Fold the white paper into a tube the same size as the inside of the glass.

2. Cut the tube to half the height of the glass. Slide the tube into the glass. From a distance it should look like a half-full glass of milk.

3. Tape the poster sideways on the wall. Use duct tape to tape the blankets and pillow to your mattress. Have one of the adults helping you tilt your mattress vertically up against the wall. Use duct tape to secure the mattress to the wall and the pillow to the bed. If the mattress keeps slipping, have an adult lie on the floor and steady it.

4. Stand 30 cm (1 foot) from the mattress. Hold the glass of "milk" sideways in your hand and have a second adult take several pictures. The picture should not show your feet.

5. Put everything back the way it was. After the film is developed, turn the photo sideways, and it will look as if you're floating on air above your bed.

MAKE LIKE AN EAGLE AT THE MALL

Even though you can't use gravitational force as a force shield, it's fun to dream about being able to control gravity. The next time you're at a mall with your friends, show them how you can flap your wings and fly. It's fun, free and fantastic.

You'll need:
- a store with a big window where you can see your reflection
- a friend who doesn't mind if you make a fool of yourself

1. Stand at the edge of a show window outside a store. Stand so half of you is reflected in the window and half is hidden.

2. Have a friend stand in front of the window and look towards you.

3. Hold up the hand and lift the leg in front of the window. Flap them up and down. Your friend will see both you and the image in the window. It will look like both halves of you are flapping like a bird and that both your legs are off the ground. It looks as if you have overcome gravity.

4. Now have your friend repeat the same procedure for you.

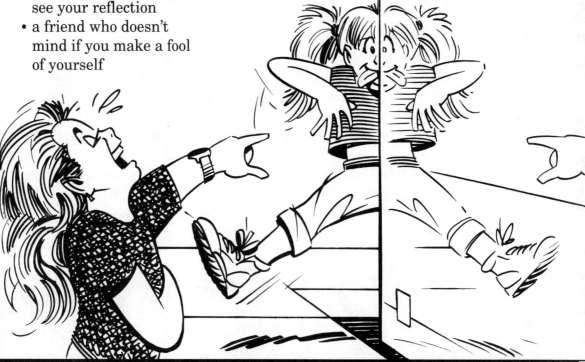

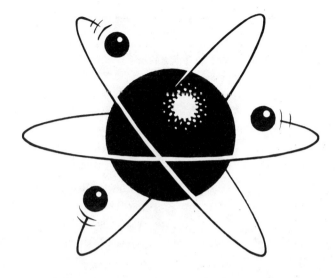

What about the two nuclear forces? These forces control what happens inside an atom. Atoms are the building blocks for practically everything in the universe. They are so small that you couldn't see them even with a microscope. An atom is made up of a positively charged nucleus around which negatively charged electrons swirl like flies around bad meat. The nucleus of an atom is made up of even smaller bits called protons and neutrons.

Since protons repel other protons, there has to be some "glue" to hold the nucleus together. That "glue" is the strong nuclear force. Even though that nuclear force is strong, it's not going to help you much in coming up with a force bubble because it acts only inside the super-tiny nucleus of an atom. The same is also true of the weak nuclear force.

So it looks like the only force you can use for a force bubble is the last of the four forces, electromagnetic force.

Electromagnetic is a word that combines both electrical and magnetic forces. The electromagnetic force is the second strongest of the four forces.

Imagine this the objects you see around you every day are all made up of billions of charges, some of them attracting, some repelling. It's like being in a tug of war on all sides, except that it's a tug of war where nobody wins.

Most of the time everything balances out and there's as much positive charge as there is negative charge in any object. But sometimes an object has extra electrons or is missing electrons. When either of these situations occur, we say that the object is electrically charged.

Two charged objects can either attract or repel each other. If one of the objects has extra electrons and the other is missing electrons, they will be attracted to each other. If they're both charged the same way, they will repel each other.

Is it possible for you to make a force bubble that uses electric forces to stop knives, guns or bullets from hitting you?

POWERBITE

When you think of making electricity, you probably think of super big generators that whirl and make strange sounds. But did you know you can make electricity by crunching a Life Saver? Electricity never tasted so good!

You'll need:
- a package of Winter-green Life Savers
- a friend who likes candy
- a dark room

1. Sit down next to each other in a dark room. Tell ghost stories until your eyes get adjusted to the darkness.

2. Watch carefully as you take a Life Saver and break it in two with your fingers. Did you see a spark? Each of you put a Life Saver in your mouth. Can you see a spark when you crunch it in two with your front teeth?

When you break the Life Saver in two, it's as if you've made static electricity and you get a spark. If you want to learn more about it, look up the word "triboluminescence" in an encyclopedia.

Suppose you're standing inside a force shield that's charged. There's only one way an electrical force bubble would work and that's if the bullets have the same charge as the force bubble. If the bullets are charged the opposite way, the bullets will be attracted to you. (Don't you hate it when that happens?) Also, if a bullet isn't charged, then it won't be affected at all by your force shield.

If an electrical force shield won't work, why not try a magnetic field? Magnetic fields deflect charged particles that are moving. But, as we've already noted, bullets probably won't have an electrical charge. They'd just pass through a magnetic field as if it weren't there.

There is one last chance. When a piece of metal, such as a bullet, enters a magnetic field, some of its electrons start to swirl around. These "eddy currents," as they're called, produce a magnetic field that fights against the original magnetic field. The result is like two magnets repelling each other. This would slow down the bullet. Only metal objects would be affected. If someone threw something at you that wasn't metal, such as a rock or an arrow, you'd be in trouble.

Let's face it—there's no way to create a force bubble with the four forces we know about. Who knows? Having a force shield might even have some disadvantages. Your best friend's dad tries to hand you a piece of cake, but the cake bounces off your force shield and falls to the floor.

"If you don't want any cake, just say so," he says. "You don't have to knock it on the floor."

"I want some. It's just that, well, this thing I invented...I can't seem to turn it off."

He frowns and cuts you another piece of cake.

This time the cake hits the force shield and bounces up to the ceiling and sticks there. You smile faintly. "Uh, sorry."

Now you know why megaheroes don't get invited out much.

WHAT ARE YOU GOING TO DO WITH ME, GORK?

I'LL DECIDE *THAT* AFTER I'VE HAD MY *BREAKFAST.* I LOVE A GOOD BREAKFAST, DON'T *YOU?*

THERE'S ONE MEGAPOWER GORK DOESN'T KNOW ABOUT—THE POWER OF *MIND OVER MATTER!* YOU GAZE AT YOUR CHAINS AND FOCUS YOUR MIND POWER ON ONE LINK... IT GLOWS DULL RED, THEN *MELTS!*

YOU STEP OUT OF YOUR CHAINS AND FOCUS YOUR MIND ON THE LOCKED CELL DOOR... IT SPRINGS *OPEN!* MOMENTS LATER, YOUR MEGAPOWERS RESTORED, YOU FIND GORK'S KITCHEN!

WONDER HOW GORK WILL LIKE HIS BREAKFAST IN THE COUNTY *JAIL?!*

For years people have claimed to have the power to read other people's minds. Even today, these "mind readers" attract large crowds. Other people claim to have the power of telekinesis, which means that they can move objects just by concentrating.

Suppose you meet the Great Fiduchi, mentalist extraordinaire. "Mr. Fiduchi," you ask, "how can you move things across the room without touching them?"

"It's a secret, kid, but would you like a demonstration? Want to see me move that vase?"

"Here's an apple I brought with me. Would you move that, please?"

Fiduchi scowls. "The aura isn't right for the apple. Are you sure you wouldn't like me to move the vase?"

"No thanks. How about moving a slice of pizza onto my plate at Joe's Pizza Place?"

"The aura is very bad in a pizza place."

"Or we could go to Ralph's grocery store and have you stack oranges."

"I can't perform my magic without preparing the auras."

"Yeah, right."

If a person can only perform on a carefully prepared stage, then it's not magic. It's more likely to be trickery.

MIND TRICKS TO PLAY ON YOUR FRIENDS

How science-minded are your friends? If they see a book move across the table, will they believe you have magic powers, or will they look for what's really causing the motion? Now's your chance to find out.

You'll need:
- string
- a telephone book
- a kitchen table
- a candle on the table
- a helper who's in on the trick

1. Tape the string to the bottom of the telephone book.

2. Run the string underneath the table to where you are sitting.

3. Tie the string to your leg.

4. Light the candle.

5. Turn out the lights and call in your family or someone else you'd like to play tricks on.

6. Say some mumbo jumbo like: "I have discovered the secrets of the ancients of Egypt. Tonight the aura is in the right phase of Androculuean (it doesn't matter how you pronounce this since it's a made-up word) hyperspace."

7. Move your leg down so that the book moves. Have your helper say, "It's a miracle!"

The laws of nature that apply to moving objects were first discovered by Isaac Newton in 1687. As far as the things we see moving around us every day, nobody's been able to improve on what he came up with.

Newton said that if an object isn't moving and the forces trying to make it go one way are exactly balanced out by the forces trying to make it go the opposite way, then the object will stay where it is. The way to get something moving is to have the forces trying to make it go one way larger than the forces trying to make it go the other way. It's sort of like, "May the strongest force win."

Simple idea, isn't it, but it works for everything from baseballs and cars to rocket ships, planets and even galaxies. That's one thing about the laws of science–they can often be written down on one sheet of paper and yet are useful for many situations.

Newton says that when the vase rises off the table and moves through the air during the Great Fiduchi's act, there must be an upward force on the vase. Probably some hard-to-see wires tied on by the Great Fiduchi himself.

Even though mind reading and telekinesis don't really exist, you can do amazing things with your mind. Did you know that your brain is better than most computers? Why? Because when a computer handles information, it does it one step at a time. But your brain, with its trillions of connections, processes information along millions of different paths at the same time.

70

MEGAMATH

How would you like to amaze your friends with your math abilities by adding up numbers faster than anyone else in your school? You'll look like you're megasmart.

Suppose you had to add up the numbers from 1 to 10. Of course you could do it the hard way–1 + 2 + 3 + 4 + 5 + 6 + 7 + 8 + 9 + 10. But here's an easier way to do it.

1. Write down the numbers from 0 to 10:

0 1 2 3 4 5 6
7 8 9 10

2. Add the first number and last numbers:
    0 + 10 = 10

3. Add the second number and the second from last:
    1 + 9 = 10

4. Keep doing this:
    2 + 8 = 10
    3 + 7 = 10
    4 + 6 = 10
You've got a 5 left over.

5. Count the number of tens you've written down:
    0 + 10 = 10
    1 + 9 = 10
    2 + 8 = 10
    3 + 7 = 10
    4 + 6 = 10
You have 5 tens.
So multiply 5 x 10, then add the 5 that was left over. The answer is 55.

What if you wanted to add the numbers from 1 to 100? Try the same solution.
    0 + 100 = 100
    1 + 99 = 100
    2 + 98 = 100
    3 + 97 = 100
    and so on

How many hundreds would you have? Fifty. What's 50 x 100? Five thousand. Plus you have a 50 left over. The answer is 5050.

I KNOW WHAT YOU'RE THINKING!

Wouldn't it be fun to amaze your friends by your ability to mind read any number from 100 to 999? You can do it–here's how.

You'll need:
• a friend who'll work with you on this trick
• a blindfold

Memorize this code used by Robert Heller, famed mentalist of the 19th century.

1 is say

2 is look or let

3 is can or can't

4 is do or don't

5 is will or won't

6 is what

7 is please

8 is are

9 is now

10 is tell

0 is hurry or come

You and your friend agree that the first word of every sentence will be a code word. For example, if the number is 346, your friend will say something like, "**C**an you see the number? **D**on't you know? **W**hat is it?"

Since you know the code, you know that "can" is three, "don't" is four and "what" is six. So you say, "The number is three hundred and forty-six."

If the number were 100, your friend might say, "Tell us the number. Hurry."

"Tell" is 10, and "hurry" is 0, so a 10 with a zero after it is 100.

Practise this trick with your friend until you can do it easily, and then during an actual performance you can ham it up using as much jargon about auras and force fields as you want.

You have a phenomenal memory, too. (Tell that to your dad the next time he reminds you that you forgot to make your bed.) But there's still room for improvement. Jerry Lucas and Harry Lorrayne have trained themselves to memorize names, faces and facts. Jerry Lucas has appeared on television several times. Before each show, he goes around meeting everyone in the audience. During the show he asks everyone to stand as he calls their names from memory!

In *The Memory Book*, Jerry Lucas and Harry Lorrayne reveal their secrets. They remember things by creating a cartoon for each name or idea they want to recall.

Suppose you want to remember ten items in order. First you need a code to help you remember. Try this one from *Blueprints for Memory* by William D. Hersey.

One   Think of fun...a roller coaster. You're in the second car of a roller coaster and the thing you want to remember is in the first car.

Two   Zoo...think of watching an elephant at the zoo.

Three Think of a tree.
Four   Think of a door.
Five   Think of going for a drive.
Six   Think of sticks.
Seven Think of heaven.
Eight Think of a gate.
Nine   Think of a sign.
Ten   Think of a hen.

Once you have this code memorized, ask friends to come up with a list of ten objects. Tell them you will be able to recite the list in any order, backwards or forwards.

Suppose the list they come up with is:
1. pancake 2. guitar 3. spoon 4. battery
5. clown 6. football 7. bee 8. pizza
9. shark 10. shoe

To memorize this list, come up with a crazy picture in your mind for each item. For example, item one is pancake. Your code for one is fun and you have fun on a roller coaster. Just imagine a giant pancake, with syrup dripping over it, sitting in front of you on a roller coaster. It's dripping on you and you can't see over it.

Item two is guitar. Your code for two is zoo and you think of an elephant. Instead of a trunk, this elephant has a guitar and sings at a rock concert.

Come up with pictures (the sillier the better) to help you remember the others. You'll be surprised how memorable things are when they're hooked onto goofy pictures.

JUST AS YOU REACH HIM, GORK JUMPS DOWN AND ZOOMS OFF ON A FAST SNOWMOBILE! YOU LET HIM GO—IF THAT CABLE *BREAKS* HUNDREDS OF PEOPLE WILL BE *KILLED!*

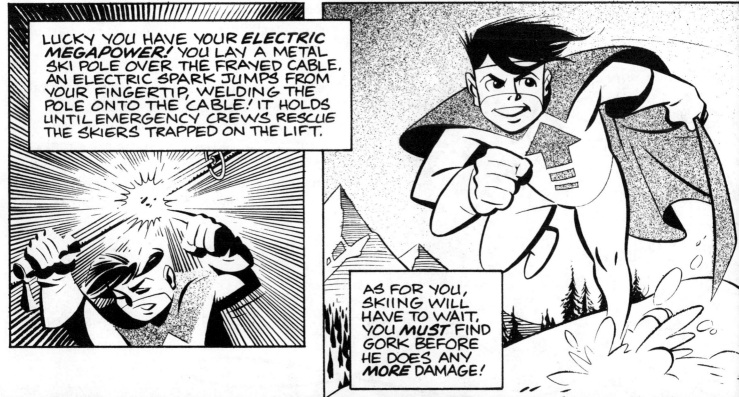

LUCKY YOU HAVE YOUR *ELECTRIC MEGAPOWER!* YOU LAY A METAL SKI POLE OVER THE FRAYED CABLE, AN ELECTRIC SPARK JUMPS FROM YOUR FINGERTIP, WELDING THE POLE ONTO THE CABLE! IT HOLDS UNTIL EMERGENCY CREWS RESCUE THE SKIERS TRAPPED ON THE LIFT.

AS FOR YOU, SKIING WILL HAVE TO WAIT, YOU *MUST* FIND GORK BEFORE HE DOES ANY *MORE* DAMAGE!

Wouldn't it be great to be able to generate electricity from your fingertips? Every time you raised your hand to answer a question at school, the teacher and the entire class would hit the floor. And think how popular you'd be during a blackout–you'd have the only working television in town!

Creatures who generate electricity aren't just on Saturday cartoons. Electric eels from South America have enough power in their tails to light up a Christmas tree–or to kill a person on contact. The surge of current is generated in cells like tiny batteries in the eel's muscles. The electric charge can be released in a fraction of a second, but it takes nearly an hour for the eel to recharge.

You generate electricity, too. In fact, you need to make electricity to keep your heart and brain functioning. A heart cell has positive and negative charges separated by its outer wall. When a nerve activates the muscle, an electric charge moves through the wall; this is what causes the muscle to contract. Every time your heart beats, one group of cells after another go through this process. The motion is a bit like football fans doing the wave.

The electrical signals that pulse through your heart muscles cause tiny electric currents that are carried to the surface of your body. These electric pulses can be monitored by connectors placed on your skin in a process called an "electrocardiogram." The "picture" produced by the electro-cardiogram tells your doctor what your heart is doing.

Your brain generates electricity, too. In fact, it uses a combination of electricity and chemistry to get a message from one part of the brain to another. First, an electrical signal travels from one end of a brain nerve cell to the other. In order to send the signal to the next nerve cell, a chemical called a neurotransmitter is used. The electrical signals produced by your brain are strong enough to be measured by a machine called an electroencephalograph. This helps doctors know what's happening in your brain.

LEMON POWER

What would you do if you were stranded on a tropical island and the batteries for your emergency radio went dead? You could grab some fruit and make a battery!

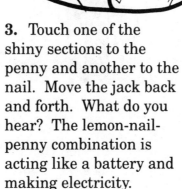

You'll need:
- a penny
- an iron nail
- a lemon
- earphones from a transistor radio

1. Stick the nail partway and the penny halfway into the lemon. The nail and the penny should be about 0.5 cm (1/4 inch) apart.

2. Put on the earphones. The end you plug into the radio is called a jack and looks like this.

The black ring is an electrical insulator; it doesn't allow electrons to flow through it.

3. Touch one of the shiny sections to the penny and another to the nail. Move the jack back and forth. What do you hear? The lemon-nail-penny combination is acting like a battery and making electricity.

4. Once you get your lemon battery working, try the same thing with a banana, potato or apple. Which one works best? Worst?

The vegetable or fruit creates a chemical reaction with the penny and the nail. Because the reaction happens at different rates for the penny and the nail, different amounts of charge build up on each. When you use the earphones to connect the nail and the penny, some of the extra charge travels from one piece of metal through the earphones to the other piece of metal. This is an electric current, which you hear as static.

The same thing happens in all batteries. You need two different kinds of metal and something to cause a chemical reaction. A battery turns chemical energy into electrical energy. When all the chemicals are used up, we say the battery is dead and it's time to get another battery.

ENLIGHTEN YOURSELF ABOUT ELECTRICITY

Get permission to take apart a flashlight.

1. Unscrew the flashlight and remove the batteries. Notice how one end of each battery has a little bump on it. Near this bump you'll see a + sign. This is the positive terminal of the battery. The other end, with the – sign, is the negative terminal of the battery.

2. With the top still off, move the on/off switch forwards and backwards. Notice that when you move the on/off switch forwards, you slide the copper strip inside the flashlight so that it touches the metallic contact near the bulb.

3. Return the batteries to the flashlight with the + end of the first next to the – end of the second one. Screw the top back

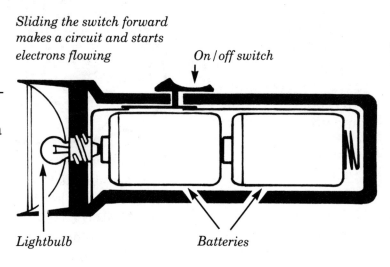

Sliding the switch forward makes a circuit and starts electrons flowing

On / off switch

Lightbulb

Batteries

on and turn on the flashlight. Does the flashlight light up? Electricity is really the flow of electrons around a complete path, called a closed circuit. By moving the copper strip forward, you've provided a complete path for the electrons. The flow of electrons around a complete path is called an electric current.

4. Unscrew the top until the light quits. Why did it quit?

5. Unscrew the top and put one battery in upside down. Screw the top back on. Does the flashlight work this way? Why not? When batteries are hooked up wrong, they fight each other. One battery wants to push electrons one way around the circuit. The other wants to push them the other way. Neither wins, so no current flows.

Suppose you were able to store up as much electricity as an eel. Would you be able to shock people? If you tried it, you'd discover that eels have it easy because they live in water. It's much harder to get electricity to travel through air than through water.

Even if you could store large amounts of electricity, you might find that so many of your cells were being used as batteries to store up the electricity that there wouldn't be enough left for walking or catching a ball or saving the world from Gork. Speaking of Gork...

You catch up to Gork just as he crashes his snowmobile into a tree. "Gork, you're coming with me to the police station."

"What happened back there at the ski lift?" he asks.

"It was an electrifying experience. You should have been there. I think it would have shocked you."

INDEX